Christmas Is Here

For Nannie and Grandpa
—L. C.

SIMON & SCHUSTER BOOKS FOR YOUNG READERS
An imprint of Simon & Schuster Children's Publishing Division
1230 Avenue of the Americas, New York, New York 10020
Illustrations copyright © 2010 by Lauren Castillo
All rights reserved, including the right of reproduction in whole or in part in any form.
SIMON & SCHUSTER BOOKS FOR YOUNG READERS is a trademark of Simon & Schuster, Inc.
For information about special discounts for bulk purchases, please contact
Simon & Schuster Special Sales at 1-866-506-1949 or business@simonandschuster.com.
The Simon & Schuster Speakers Bureau can bring authors to your live event.
For more information or to book an event, contact the Simon & Schuster Speakers Bureau
at 1-866-248-3049 or visit our website at www.simonspeakers.com.
Book design by Laurent Linn
The text for this book is set in Aunt Mildred.
The illustrations for this book are rendered in ink, watercolor, and acetone transfer.
Manufactured in China
0610 SCP
2 4 6 8 10 9 7 5 3 1
Library of Congress Cataloging-in-Publication Data
Bible. N.T. Luke II, 8-14. English. Authorized. 2010.
Christmas is here : words from the King James Bible / illustrated by
Lauren Castillo.—1st ed.
p. cm.
ISBN 978-1-4424-0822-7 (hardcover)
1. Jesus Christ—Nativity—Juvenile literature. 2. Christmas—Juvenile literature.
I. Castillo, Lauren. II. Title.
BT315.A3 2010
232.92—dc22
2009045979

Christmas
Is Here

Words from the
KING JAMES BIBLE

Illustrated by
LAUREN CASTILLO

SIMON & SCHUSTER BOOKS FOR YOUNG READERS

New York   London   Toronto   Sydney

And there were in the same country
shepherds abiding in the field,

keeping watch over their flock by night.

And, lo, the angel of the Lord came upon them,

and the glory of the Lord
shone round about them;

and they were sore afraid.

And the angel said unto them, "Fear not:
for, behold, I bring you good tidings of
great joy, which shall be to all people.

"For unto you is born this day in the city
of David, a Savior, which is Christ the Lord.

"And this shall be a sign unto you;

"Ye shall find the babe wrapped in
swaddling clothes, lying in a manger."

And suddenly there was with the angel a
multitude of the heavenly host, praising God,

and saying, "Glory to God in the highest,

"and on earth peace,
good will toward men."